THE CIVIL WAR

THE CIVIL WAR

by ANNE DEVEREAUX JORDAN

with VIRGINIA SCHOMP

 Marshall Cavendish
Benchmark
New York

For Kathy Benson, and in fond memory of James Haskins

❖❖

The authors and publisher are grateful to Jill Watts, professor of history at California State University, San Marcos, for her perceptive comments on the manuscript, and to the late Richard Newman, civil rights advocate, author, and senior research officer at the W. E. B. DuBois Institute at Harvard University, for his excellent work in formulating the series.

EDITOR: JOYCE STANTON   EDITORIAL DIRECTOR: MICHELLE BISSON
ART DIRECTOR: ANAHID HAMPARIAN   SERIES DESIGNER: MICHAEL NELSON

MARSHALL CAVENDISH BENCHMARK 99 WHITE PLAINS ROAD TARRYTOWN, NEW YORK 10591-9001
www.marshallcavendish.us Text copyright © 2007 by Anne Devereaux Jordan All rights reserved. No part of this book may be reproduced or utilized in any form or by any means electronic or mechanical including photocopying, recording, or by any information storage and retrieval system, without permission from the copyright holders. All Internet sites were available and accurate when this book was sent to press. LIBRARY OF CONGRESS CATALOGING-IN-PUBLICATION DATA: Jordan, Anne Devereaux. The Civil War / by Anne Devereaux Jordan ; with Virginia Schomp. p. cm. — (Drama of African-American history) Summary: "Describes the role of African Americans during the Civil War (1861-1865)"—Provided by publisher. Includes bibliographical references and index. ISBN-13: 978-0-7614-2179-5 ISBN-10: 0-7614-2179-3 1. United States—History—Civil War, 1861-1865—African Americans—Juvenile literature. 2. United States—History—Civil War, 1861-1865—Participation, African American—Juvenile literature. 3. African Americans—History—To 1863—Juvenile literature. 4. African Americans—History—1863-1877—Juvenile literature. 5. African American soldiers—History—19th century—Juvenile literature. I. Schomp, Virginia. II. Title. III. Series. E540.N3J67 2007 973.7089'96073—dc22 2006012472

Images provided by Rose Corbett Gordon, Art Editor, Mystic CT, from the following sources: Cover: Scala/Art Resource, NY Back cover: Corbis Page i: Library of Congress/Bridgeman Art Library; pages ii - iii: The Art Archive/Metropolitan Museum of Art, NY/Laurie Platt Winfrey; pages vii, 4, 8, 43, 44, 60: The Art Archive/Culver Pictures; pages viii, 6, 10, 12, 14, 33, 42, 51 top & bottom, 65: Bettmann/Corbis; page 3: The Art Archive/Oakland Museum/Laurie Platt Winfrey; pages 7, 15, 19, 21, 24, 26, 47, 52, 56, 64: Corbis; page 9: Chicago Historical Society; page 27: Medford Historical Society/Corbis; page 30 top: National Portrait Gallery, Smithsonian Institution/Art Resource, NY; page 30 bottom: Courtesy of the Yale University Library; page 32: The Art Archive; page 34: Christie's Images/Corbis; page 36: Massachusetts Historical Society, Boston/Bridgeman Art Library; page 39: Beinecke Rare Book and Manuscript Library, Yale University; page 48: Private Collection/Bridgeman Art Library; page 53: James A. Chambers/US Army/Deputy. Office of the Chief, Military Intelligence; page 54: The Art Archive/Private Collection; pages 58, 62: Library of Congress

—— A NOTE ON LANGUAGE ——

In order to preserve the character and historical accuracy of the quoted material appearing in this book, we have not corrected or modernized spellings, capitalization, punctuation, or grammar. We have also retained the "dialect spelling" that was sometimes used by white writers in an attempt to reproduce the way some former slaves spoke. You will occasionally come across words such as *colored* and *Negro*, which were commonly used by both white Americans and African Americans in Civil War times.

Printed in China
1 3 5 6 4 2

Front cover: African-American troops with their white officer at a military camp in Pennsylvania
Back cover: Children at a "contraband school" for former slaves
Half-title page: A black soldier in the Union army
Title page: Escaped slaves make a desperate journey north toward freedom.

CONTENTS

INTRODUCTION

The Civil War is the fourth book in the series Drama of African-American History. Earlier books in this series have explored the journey of captive Africans to the Americas and the development of slavery in the United States. Now we will learn how the issue of slavery divided North and South, leading to a deadly struggle over the future of the young nation.

The institution of slavery was introduced into North America in early colonial times. It gradually died out in the North, where it proved unprofitable in the region's many small farms and industries. Meanwhile, in the South, slavery put down deep roots. There slave labor became the foundation of an economy built on large plantations where cotton, tobacco, and other crops were grown.

Many Northerners believed that slavery was wrong. They hoped that it would eventually disappear from the South, and they were determined to keep it from spreading into the new territories opening up in the American West. A small but vocal minority of Northerners were abolitionists. Many abolitionists not only denounced slavery but also called for the federal government to end it immediately and completely.

The South also had its abolitionists. In fact, in the early 1800s, there were more antislavery societies in the South than in the North. The great majority of white Southerners did not even own slaves. Many of these nonslaveholders considered human bondage sinful. They also worried about the possibility of a violent uprising by the millions of enslaved people in their midst.

By the 1830s, however, the Southern antislavery movement had almost completely faded. As plantations became more and more dependent on slave labor, Southerners became convinced that freeing the slaves would destroy their region's economy. Several small but bloody slave rebellions made Southern whites more determined than ever to control the black population. In addition, fierce attacks by Northern abolitionists made all Southerners angry and defensive. Whatever their differences, slaveholders and nonslaveholders could agree on one point: Northerners had no right telling them how to run their half of the country.

Another major factor in the growing division between North and South was politics. The booming population of the Northern states was boosting that region's political influence. Northern legislators had already gained a majority in the House of Representatives. If slavery was barred from the West, the antislavery forces would gain control of the Senate, too. That could leave Southerners at the mercy of a government that was hostile to their rights and interests. In a fiery speech to Congress, Senator Jefferson Davis of Mississippi accused Northern lawmakers of opposing the spread of slavery to increase their own power. "It is not humanity that influences you," Davis roared. "It is that you may have a majority in the Congress of the United States and convert the Government into an engine of Northern aggrandizement. . . . [You] want by an unjust system of legislation to promote the industry of the United States at the expense of the people of the South."

As the slavery debate grew ever more heated, the positions of North and South hardened. Some Americans even began to wonder if a single government could represent two peoples with such different points of view. In 1848 Maryland plantation owner Sidney George Fisher reflected on the "alarming" developments. "There is great reason to fear," Fisher wrote, "that ere long there will be a Northern party and a Southern party. . . . When the question comes to be fairly raised—which shall govern, South or North—then the Union will be in imminent danger."

Above: Charity Still twice escaped from slavery. The second time, in 1807, she succeeded.

U.S. statesman Henry Clay tried to resolve the conflict over the spread of slavery with the Missouri Compromise of 1820.

Chapter 1

A HOUSE DIVIDED

AMERICA'S FIRST MAJOR POLITICAL CRISIS OVER SLAVERY came in 1819. The conflict centered on the question of extending slavery into the western territories acquired in the Louisiana Purchase of 1803. The territory of Missouri had requested statehood. Northerners wanted it to enter the Union as a free state, while Southerners were equally determined that Missouri should have slaves. The debate was especially heated because, at the time, there were eleven slave states and eleven free states, and Missouri would upset that delicate balance.

Congress ended the standoff with a compromise proposed by Kentucky representative Henry Clay. Under the Missouri Compromise of 1820, Missouri became a slave state and Maine was admitted into the Union as a free state. A geographical line was drawn along Missouri's southern border, stretching through the Louisiana Territory. Land to the south of the line would be slave territory, and land to the north would be free.

With the Missouri Compromise line fixing the limits of slavery, the dispute over the western territories subsided. But a troubling question remained. What would happen when new areas of North America opened up to settlement? To former president Thomas Jefferson, "this momentous question" was like "a fire bell in the night [that] awakened and filled me with terror. . . . It is hushed, indeed for the moment. But this is a reprieve only, not a final sentence."

THE COMPROMISE OF 1850

Within three decades of the Missouri Compromise, Thomas Jefferson's prediction would prove accurate. The line that had resolved the Missouri crisis would become the basis of an even more bitter conflict. And that conflict would usher in one of the most divisive periods in American history.

The new controversy began with a major expansion of U.S. territory. In 1848 the United States won the Mexican-American War and gained more than one million square miles in the Southwest. Those lands included all or parts of what would become the states of California, New Mexico, Arizona, Colorado, Nevada, Utah, and Wyoming.

The war had barely ended when the argument over slavery in the new lands began. Some Americans wanted to extend the Missouri Compromise line through the Southwest all the way to the Pacific Ocean. Others proposed that the citizens of each territory decide the issue of slavery for themselves. Abolitionists wanted to abolish slavery throughout the United States, while some Southerners argued that the federal government did

not have the right to ban slavery anywhere. The many-sided dispute took on added urgency when gold was discovered in California. By 1850, nearly 100,000 people had made their way to California, hoping to strike it rich in the gold rush. With these settlers clamoring for statehood, Congress had to agree on a policy for the Southwest.

Prospectors dream of striking it rich in the California gold rush. California's rapid growth led to heated debates over the westward expansion of slavery.

Once again it was Kentucky representative Henry Clay who worked out a compromise. The complicated set of bills that Clay presented to Congress had something for everyone. To satisfy Northerners, the slave trade would be banned in Washington, DC, and California would enter the Union as a free state. To win Southern support, Clay proposed to allow the citizens of the other territories to decide for themselves whether to permit or ban slavery. Also included in his proposal was a strict new Fugitive Slave Act, which would make it easier for slave owners to recapture slaves who escaped to free states and territories.

Congress approved the Compromise of 1850 by a narrow margin. Many Americans hoped that this would put the slavery question to rest once and for all. Instead, the compromise brought only a brief calm before the terrible storm that was gathering.

UNCLE TOM'S CABIN

The most controversial part of the Compromise of 1850 was the Fugitive Slave Act. Under this new law, African Americans who were accused of being runaway slaves were denied the right to speak in their own defense. That made it easy for fugitives to be returned to slavery and, even worse, for free blacks to be enslaved. Northerners were especially angered by provisions in the law that not only required all citizens to help slaveholders capture suspected runaways but also made it a federal crime to assist an escaped slave.

Abolitionist Harriet Beecher Stowe was so outraged by the Fugitive Slave Act that she decided to write an antislavery novel. *Uncle Tom's Cabin,* published in 1852, dramatized the suffering of slaves and the cruelty of slaveholders. The novel became an immediate best seller. It converted thousands of Northerners to the antislavery cause and infuriated countless Southerners, who denounced it as a pack of lies and attempted to ban the book. Many people believed that Stowe's book helped start the Civil War by inflaming passions on both sides. Abraham Lincoln shared that view. According to some accounts, when the president met Harriet Beecher Stowe a decade after the publication of *Uncle Tom's Cabin,* he said, "So this is the little lady who wrote the book that made this great war."

Above: Harriet Beecher Stowe believed that the Union could only be saved "by repentance, justice and mercy."

"Bleeding Kansas"

In 1854 Senator Stephen Douglas of Illinois proposed that Congress open a large area of the Great Plains to settlement. The region would be divided into two parts, Kansas Territory and Nebraska Territory. Under the Missouri Compromise, these territories should be free. In order to win Southern support for his proposal, however, Douglas wanted to repeal the Missouri Compromise and allow territorial settlers to decide the issue of slavery for themselves.

After a long debate, Congress approved Douglas's plan, which was known as the Kansas-Nebraska Act. The result was chaos. Northerners and Southerners battled fiercely over the control of Kansas, the more southern of the two new territories. Slaveholders from the neighboring state of Missouri rushed to build proslavery settlements in Kansas. Northern abolitionists organized groups of "Free-Soil" settlers, who raced to stake their own claims. Clashes between the two groups soon led to violence.

In May 1856 a group of Missourians who supported slavery crossed the border and raided the Free-Soil town of Lawrence, Kansas. The "Border Ruffians" beat up settlers, ransacked homes and stores, and smashed the town's two printing presses. A few days later, Kansas settler John Brown retaliated. The fiery abolitionist led a small band of supporters in an attack on a proslavery settlement on Pottawatomie Creek, murdering five settlers.

The attacks marked the beginning of open warfare. In the following months, hundreds of people were killed in fighting between the pro- and antislavery factions in "Bleeding Kansas." Southerners applauded the actions of the Border

Ruffians. Northerners praised John Brown and the other Free-Soilers. Reflecting on the growing divisions between North and South, abolitionist leader William Lloyd Garrison was encouraged by

> the change affected in public opinion . . . a change so great indeed, that whereas, ten years [ago], there were thousands who could not endure my lightest word of [criticism] of the South, they can now easily swallow John Brown whole and his rifle into the bargain. In firing his gun, he has merely told us what time of day it is. It is high noon, thank God!

THE DRED SCOTT CASE

The gap between North and South grew even wider in 1857, with a landmark legal decision. The case involved a slave named Dred Scott. Born into slavery in Virginia, Scott had been sold to an army surgeon in Missouri. He had accompanied his master to army posts in Illinois and Wisconsin, where slavery was prohibited under the Missouri Compromise. After the surgeon died in 1843, Scott came under the control of the man's brother-in-law,

THE CIVIL WAR

John Sanford. Three years later, Scott sued for his freedom, arguing that he had become free when he lived on free soil.

Over the next ten years, the case of *Dred Scott* v. *Sanford* dragged through one court after another. Finally, it reached the United States Supreme Court. In March 1857 the Court handed down its decision. According to a majority of the justices, slaves and their descendants were not U.S. citizens and therefore did not have the right to sue in federal court. Further, since the Constitution had recognized slavery, Congress had no right to exclude it from any territory.

Southerners were overjoyed by the Dred Scott decision, which not only upheld their right to slave "property" but also overturned the Missouri Compromise. Black Americans felt angry and discouraged. Abolitionist leader Frederick Douglass, who had escaped from slavery, blasted the decision and urged his fellow African Americans not to give up their dreams of freedom and equality. "Such a decision cannot stand," Douglass vowed. "This very attempt to blot out forever the hopes of an enslaved people may be one necessary link in the chain of events preparatory to the downfall and complete overthrow of the whole slave system."

The Dred Scott decision was front-page news. This New York paper featured illustrations of Scott and his family.

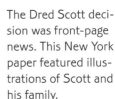

JOHN BROWN'S RAID

Abolitionist John Brown hoped to "effect a mighty conquest" over slavery with his raid on Harpers Ferry.

On the night of October 16, 1859, abolitionist John Brown and a small band of followers raided the federal arsenal at Harpers Ferry, Virginia. Brown's tiny army consisted of five black men and sixteen white men. They planned to seize weapons and ammunition and give them to slaves in the area. Brown hoped that this would spark a widespread slave uprising, striking a deadly blow against slavery throughout the South.

At first, all went as planned. Brown and his men subdued the arsenal's guards without firing a shot. They seized the weapons and began distributing them to the slaves on neighboring plantations. However, they failed to capture the rest of the village, and they allowed a train to leave the station, carrying word of the rebellion down the line. By the following morning, hordes of armed white townspeople, farmers, militiamen, and soldiers were pouring into Harpers Ferry. John Brown was captured, and all but five of his men were taken or killed. Four townspeople and a U.S. marine were also killed in the fighting.

John Brown was tried and convicted of murder, conspiracy, and treason against the state of Virginia. On December 2, 1859, he rode his own coffin on a wagon to the gallows. Just before he was hanged, the defiant abolitionist handed one of his guards a note: "I, John Brown, am now quite certain that the crimes of this guilty land will never be purged away but with blood."

The actions of John Brown and his raiders left the South badly shaken. Convinced that the abolitionists would stop at nothing in their battle against slavery, Southern militias began

Charlestown, Va, 2 December 1859.

I John Brown am now quite certain that the crimes of this guilty land: will never be purged away; but with Blood. I had as I now think: vainly flattered myself that without very much bloodshed; it might be done.

John Brown's last note, handed to a guard on the morning of his execution

to drill in preparation for slave rebellions and battles with Northern foes. Meanwhile, to many Northerners, John Brown became a hero of the antislavery cause. On the day of his execution, free African Americans gathered in Northern cities to honor their fallen champion and cry out against slavery. Black abolitionist Frances Ellen Watkins thanked Brown "in the name of the slave mother, her heart rocked to and fro by the agony of her mournful separations. . . . I hope that from your sad fate great good may arise to the cause of freedom."

THE ELECTION OF ABRAHAM LINCOLN

"The day of compromise is past," proclaimed a South Carolina newspaper. "There is no peace for the South in the Union." John Brown's raid had added fuel to the controversy raging between North and South. As the presidential election of 1860 drew near, tensions were reaching the boiling point.

There were four major candidates competing for the presidency. Northern Democrats had nominated Illinois senator Stephen Douglas, the author of the Kansas-Nebraska Act. Douglas was a moderate who believed that the question of slavery should be left up to each territory or state to decide.

Southern Democrats had split with their party and nominated John C. Breckinridge of Kentucky, who pledged to actively support slavery in the western territories. A small group of Southern Democrats had formed their own party, choosing a more conservative proslavery candidate, John Bell of Tennessee. The fourth candidate, the nominee of the Republican Party, was Illinois lawyer and former congressman Abraham Lincoln.

Lincoln was a moderate who promised to leave slavery alone where it already existed but to halt its further spread. He was convinced that the federal government did not have the authority to act against slavery in the Southern states. He also believed that slavery was morally wrong, and he hoped that it would gradually die out if it was confined to the South. In an 1858 speech, he had quoted a line from the Bible in presenting his vision of a nation where slavery was set "in the course of ultimate extinction."

The Republican candidate for the presidency in 1860 was a personable lawyer known as "Honest Abe" Lincoln.

"A house divided against itself cannot stand." I believe this government cannot endure, permanently half slave and half free. I do not expect the Union to be dissolved—I do not expect the house to fall—but I do expect it will cease to be divided. It will become all one thing, or all the other.

White Southerners felt threatened by Lincoln's antislavery statements. Despite his assurances, they feared that the Republican candidate intended to move against slavery in the South.

If Lincoln was elected, some Southern leaders maintained, they would have no choice but to secede, or withdraw from the Union.

In November 1860 Abraham Lincoln won the presidency with just 40 percent of the popular vote, carrying nearly the entire North but not a single state in the South. Republicans celebrated their triumph with parades, speeches, and bonfires. Meanwhile, Southerners lit their own flames. In towns and cities throughout the South, Lincoln was burned in effigy. A Virginia newspaper called the Republican victory "undoubtedly the greatest evil that has ever befallen this country." To one Alabama congressman, the election was "a declaration of war against our property and the supremacy of the white race."

African Americans had a ready answer for the growing ranks of Southerners calling for secession. "Go at once," declared former slave H. Ford Douglass. "There is no union of ideas and interests in this country, and there can be no union between freedom and slavery."

Chapter 2

CONTRABANDS OF WAR

WITHIN A FEW WEEKS OF ABRAHAM LINCOLN'S election, the nation was falling apart. On December 20, 1860, South Carolina seceded from the Union. By the following February, six other Southern states had followed. The seceded states formed an independent nation, the Confederate States of America.

Lincoln was sworn in as president on March 4, 1861. In his inaugural address, he vowed to preserve the Union and protect U.S. government property. The Confederates responded on April 12 by attacking and capturing Fort Sumter in South Carolina. Lincoln called for 75,000 volunteer soldiers to suppress the rebellion. Four more Southern states took up arms for the Confederacy. The Civil War had begun.

Opposite: Confederate cannons pound Fort Sumter at the start of the Civil War.

REACHING FOR FREEDOM

"My Dear Wife," wrote John Boston, a runaway slave from Maryland, "it is with grate joy I take this time to let you know Whare I am i am now in Safety in the 14th Regiment of Brooklyn this Day I can Adress you thank god as a free man."

At the start of the Civil War, the great majority of white Northerners viewed the conflict strictly as a battle to save the Union. African Americans had a different goal. From the moment Northern troops set foot on Southern soil, captive black men and women began to run toward freedom. Like John Boston, thousands of slaves escaped from their masters in the early months of the war, seeking refuge within Union lines. Most of the fugitives came from the slaveholding states on the border between North and South, which included

Fugitive slaves cross a river in Virginia. Slaves who found refuge behind Union lines were regarded as "contrabands of war."

Delaware, Kentucky, Maryland, Missouri, and Virginia. With the exception of Virginia, the border states had remained loyal to the Union.

These fugitive slaves posed a serious problem for U.S. military commanders. Hoping to retain the support of the loyal Southern states, the president and Congress had promised to respect slaveholders'

THE CIVIL WAR

property rights. At first, army commanders tried to uphold that policy. Many officers banished runaway slaves from the Union camps. Some even sent the fugitives back to their masters under armed guard.

No matter how many people the army turned away, however, the fugitives just kept coming. Soon their persistence forced Union commanders to rethink their policies. The first big change came at Fortress Monroe, a large military base near Hampton, Virginia, that had remained under Union control. In May 1861 three slaves who had been laboring on Confederate fortifications escaped to Fortress Monroe. The fort's commander, Union general Benjamin Butler, decided not to return the runaways to their master. Instead, he labeled them "contrabands of war," or property of military value seized from the enemy. Then he put them to work for his own forces. In a report to his superiors, the general asked, "Shall [the Confederates] be allowed the use of property against the United States and we not be allowed its use in aid of the United States?"

Union general Benjamin F. Butler championed the rights of African Americans during and after the Civil War.

A few days later, Butler wrote again, reporting that not only male slaves who had been working for the Confederates but entire families were now making their way to Fortress Monroe. The general had decided to put all the able-bodied fugitives to work and issue food rations to laborers and nonlaborers alike. "As a military question," he wrote, depriving the Confederates of slave labor "would seem to be a matter of necessity. . . .

As a political question and a question of humanity can I receive the services of a Father and Mother and not take the children?"

The army approved General Butler's actions. Soon other Union officers began taking in fugitives. Within a few months, tens of thousands of refugees had taken shelter at makeshift "contraband camps" established throughout Union-held territory.

In August 1861 the U.S. Congress passed the First Confiscation Act. The law gave the army the authority to confiscate all property, including slaves, that might be used "in hostile service against the Government of the United States." Nearly a year later, the Second Confiscation Act forbade Union officers to return fugitives to Confederate masters. By the war's end, an estimated 500,000 escaped slaves would find shelter within Union lines. Many other fugitives would gather in cities, towns, and rural settlements in areas of the South occupied by the Union army.

CHANGING MINDS

Most Northern soldiers approved of sheltering fugitive slaves. It seemed foolish to return the runaways to masters who would put them to work for the Confederate cause. Besides, the contrabands provided valuable services to the army, working as laborers, blacksmiths, carpenters, teamsters, cooks, laundresses, personal servants, hospital attendants, scouts, spies, and guides. One Northern soldier stationed in the South explained that his regiment employed contrabands as "teamsters and cooks, which puts that many more men back in the ranks. . . . It will make a difference in [this regiment] of not less than 75 men that will carry guns that did not before." In Union-occupied parts of North Carolina, Northern missionary Vincent Colyer reported

SUSIE KING TAYLOR

In November 1861 the Union army invaded the South Carolina Sea Islands. Confederate plantation owners fled, leaving behind about ten thousand slaves. Northern abolitionists and missionaries took up the challenge of aiding all these contrabands. Within a few months, hundreds of volunteers, black and white, had come to the islands to start schools, hospitals, and churches. Among the teachers was fourteen-year-old Susie King Taylor, who had secretly learned to read and write while growing up as a slave in Georgia. In this passage from her autobiography, Susie described her excitement in the early days of the war, when she first learned about the Union troops bringing the promise of freedom.

I had been reading so much about the "Yankees" I was very anxious to see them. The whites would tell their colored people not to go to the Yankees, for they would harness them to carts and make them pull the carts around, in place of horses. I asked grandmother, one day, if this was true. She replied, "Certainly not!" that the white people did not want slaves to go over to the Yankees, and told them these things to frighten them. . . . I wanted to see these wonderful "Yankees" so much, as I heard my parents say the Yankee was going to set all the slaves free. Oh, how these people prayed for freedom! . . .

On April 1, 1862, about the time the Union soldiers were firing on Fort Pulaski [in Georgia], I was sent out into the country to my mother. I remember what a roar and din the guns made. They jarred the earth for miles. The fort was at last taken by them. Two days after the taking of Fort Pulaski, my uncle took his family of seven and myself to St. Catherine Island [in the Sea Islands]. We landed under the protection of the Union fleet, and . . . at last, to my unbounded joy, I saw the "Yankee."

that contrabands "were kept constantly employed on the perilous but most important duty of spies, scouts and guides." These "most courageous" volunteers "frequently went from thirty to three hundred miles within the enemy's lines . . . bringing us back important reliable information."

Some Union soldiers not only recognized the value of contraband labor but were also moved by the slaves' fierce longing for freedom. The war had brought these Northerners face-to-face with slaves and slaveholders for the first time in their lives. Even soldiers who opposed abolition sometimes changed their minds after witnessing the brutalities of the slave system. A Union commander serving in Maryland reported that slaveholders who "obtained possession of their slaves . . . immediately set to work flogging them in view of the troops." Disgusted by these barbaric acts, the soldiers "would go out and rescue the Negro, and in some instances would thrash the masters."

Behind Union Lines

While life in the contraband camps was nearly always better than life on the plantations, fugitive slaves still faced many difficulties. They were not legally free but not exactly slaves. Most were completely dependent on the Union army for food, clothing, shelter, and security. Many Northern officers and soldiers remained hostile to blacks. As a result, contrabands might be underpaid, overworked, or even physically abused.

At Fortress Monroe fugitive slaves employed by the army were credited with wages of ten dollars a month. However, nearly all of that money went into a fund to support contrabands who were unfit for military labor, such as children, women with small children, and the elderly. In Helena,

Arkansas, officers reported that contrabands who had been paid for their labor were often "waylaid by soldiers, robbed, and in several cases fired upon." Near New Orleans, Louisiana, former slaves were forced to work seven days a week repairing earthen dams. In return, the army lodged them in a filthy old barn and issued meager food and clothing rations. "My cattle at home are better cared for than these unfortunate persons," observed one Northern officer.

To prevent such abuses, Union commanders appointed superintendents to oversee the employment of the people in the contraband camps. Under the direction of the superintendents, some former slaves continued to work for the army, while others were hired out to white employers for wages. As the army

Many former slaves learned to read and write at schools set up in contraband camps.

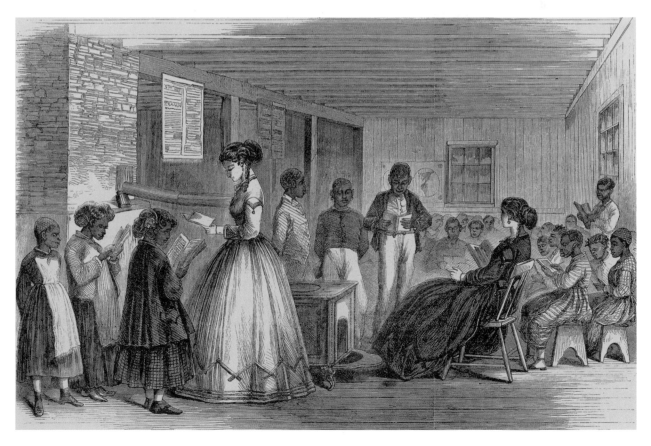

moved deeper into the South, contrabands also found paid employment on plantations that had been confiscated by the federal government. A few managed to buy or rent their own small plots of land. No matter how or where they worked, all these former slaves experienced the satisfaction of supporting themselves through their own efforts and talents.

Further help for the contrabands came from freedmen's aid societies organized by Northern abolitionists, churches, and charities. The societies provided food, clothing, medicine, and other supplies. Most importantly, they gave former slaves their first chance for an education. Under Southern laws it was illegal to teach a slave to read or write. Consequently, more than 90 percent of slaves were illiterate. To help these people make the transition from slavery to freedom, the aid societies established schools in small towns, large cities, and former plantations throughout the South. By the war's end, an estimated 200,000 Southern black men, women, and children had learned to read at the contraband schools.

Left Behind

For every slave who escaped from bondage during the Civil War, several more remained behind Confederate lines. Some were too young, old, or frail to attempt flight. Some lived too far from the occupying Union forces. Many slaves feared the harsh punishments they would suffer if they were recaptured or worried about the loved ones they would be forced to leave behind.

Most African Americans who remained in slavery continued to work on plantations, producing food and clothing not only for their masters but for the Confederate troops, too. Slaves also dug trenches, built forts, and drove wagons for the

Gunmen patrol a Southern road, checking passes to make sure slaves have permission to leave their masters' property.

Confederacy. In addition, some slaveholders who joined the army brought along a trusted slave to act as a personal servant.

For the slaves who remained on Southern farms and plantations, life grew even grimmer during the war years. When slaveholders marched off to war, they sometimes left the management of their slaves to a hired overseer. These new managers often used harsh discipline in an attempt to maintain order. In many Southern communities, armed patrols known as home guards helped keep an eye on slaves' movements and crush signs of unrest and resistance. The Confederate army also helped protect the slave system. "There is a great disposition among the Negroes to be insubordinate [defiant]," reported one Confederate officer in Mississippi. "Within the last 12 months we have had to hang some 40 for plotting an insurrection, and there has been about that number put in irons."

Some plantation owners tried to hold on to their valuable "property" by taking their slaves to areas far from the Union lines. Others made a quick profit by selling their slaves to buyers in the Deep South. As Union forces approached, owners might even threaten to kill all their slaves rather than grant them freedom. Katie Rowe of Arkansas never forgot the day her master gathered his slaves together and "tell us de law!"

> "You . . . been seeing de 'Federate soldiers coming by here looking purty raggedy and hurt and wore out," he say, "but dat no sign dey licked! Dem Yankees ain't gwine git dis fur, but iffen dey do you all ain't gwine git free by 'em, 'cause I gwine free you befo' dat. When dey git here dey going find you already free, 'cause I gwine line you up . . . and free you wid my shotgun! Anybody miss jest one lick wid de hoe, . . . and he gwine be free and talking to de devil long befo' he ever see a pair of blue britches!"

In some cases, however, enslaved African Americans found that the Civil War brought them greater control over their lives than ever before. When only the mistress and her children were left to manage a plantation, the slave system often fell apart. Isaac Adams, who was born a slave in Louisiana, recalled that "they wasn't anybody at our place but the womenfolks and the negroes. . . . They wasn't no place to go, anyway, so [the slaves] all stayed on. But they didn't do very much work. Just enough to take care of themselves and their whitefolks."

In the border states, plantation owners sometimes had to negotiate with their laborers to keep them from fleeing to nearby Union camps. Many slaves managed to force their masters to relax restrictions and grant new privileges, including wages. According to one report, planters in Rutherford County, Tennessee, "with the view of securing the services of their slaves—or in other words to . . . prevent them from running away—have promised to give them 10 cts [cents] per lb [pound] for all the cotton they may produce."

Chapter 3

Forever Free

WHILE THE CIVIL WAR BEGAN AS A BATTLE FOR AND against Southern independence, it was slavery that had divided Northerners and Southerners and forced them to settle their differences with blood. Even so, both sides agreed that the struggle was between white citizens. Black Americans, free or enslaved, would play no role in the fight.

But African Americans would not be ignored. To them, it was clear that a war to defeat Southern secession and save the Union must sooner or later become a battle against slavery. By fleeing their masters and seeking refuge behind Union army lines, the contrabands made themselves a military and political issue. By working for the Union cause, both contrabands and free blacks strengthened their claims to freedom. And by insisting on the right to fight for their country,

Opposite: From the start of the Civil War, black men pressed for a chance to serve their country in the fight for freedom.

African Americans would gradually force white Northerners to embrace emancipation.

A "White Man's War"

From the first shots of the Civil War, African Americans volunteered to fight. Black men flooded Union army recruiting stations in the North. They wrote to military commanders and petitioned state governments, asking for the repeal of laws that barred them from serving in the militias. Many black communities formed military companies and began regular combat drills.

Volunteers line up to join the Union army. It would take months of hard fighting before the army agreed to black enlistment.

All these offers of assistance were rejected. President Lincoln and the other Union leaders were afraid that arming blacks would offend slaveholders in the loyal border states as well as Northerners who opposed abolition. Like most whites in both the North and South, Lincoln also believed that former slaves were not smart enough or brave enough to make good soldiers. "If we were to arm them," the president told the supporters of black enlistment, "I fear that in a few weeks the arms would be in the hands of the rebels." A white volunteer aiding contrabands in the South Carolina Sea Islands agreed. "Negroes—plantation negroes, at least—will never make soldiers in one generation," he wrote. "Five white men could put a regiment to flight."

As a result of this widespread prejudice, free African Americans who tried to enlist were turned away and black military companies were ordered to disband. In New York City, an angry white mob threatened black men engaged in combat drills. In Cincinnati, Ohio, a policeman told a group of would-be soldiers, "We want you damned [blacks] to keep out of this; this is a white man's war."

Northern blacks who were denied the right to fight often found other ways to aid the Union war effort. Some light-skinned black men "passed" as white and enlisted in all-white regiments. Other free African Americans took jobs working for the army. The *Afro-American* newspaper of Washington, DC, reported in late 1861 that the city's black men and women were busy attending to war business.

Numbers of our young men [cook] for officers' messes. . . . Others attend exclusively to the horses of army officers. . . . Many are engaged at the rail-road depot unloading and storing the immense amount of freight that daily arrives here from the North and West. Three or four thousand men are employed at cutting wood in Virginia around the different fortifications. . . . Laundresses are doing a fine business. They have the exclusive wash of entire regiments. . . . None need be idle.

The first black enlisted men served as manual laborers or servants to white officers.

Even as they worked for Union victory, African Americans continued to call for black enlistment. They knew that the war offered an exceptional opportunity to strike a blow against slavery and strengthen their claim to equality. "If ever colored men plead[ed] for rights or fought for liberty, now of all others is the time," wrote Alfred Green, an African-American schoolteacher in Philadelphia. "God will help no one that refuses to help himself. . . . The prejudiced white men North or South never will respect us until they are forced to do it by deeds of our own."

DOUBTS AND DELAYS

During the early months of the Civil War, the North suffered a series of military defeats. As hopes of a quick and glorious victory faded, fewer and fewer white men volunteered to join the army. More troops were desperately needed, but President Lincoln and other government leaders still feared that enlisting black soldiers would erode support for the war.

Union commanders facing Confederate forces were more interested in action than politics. In late 1861 many commanders began to fill out their dwindling ranks with volunteers from the contraband camps. A few generals actively recruited runaway slaves and formed unauthorized black regiments, which included both volunteers and men who were forced into service. The federal government, still wavering over the question of black enlistment, ignored some of the new regiments and condemned others. In mid-1862, for example, the Department of War forced General David Hunter to disband his all-black First South Carolina Volunteer Regiment. A few weeks later, General Rufus Saxton was authorized to reorganize the regiment, and another general received permission to enlist free blacks in Louisiana.

In July 1862 the Second Confiscation Act empowered the president to "employ as many persons of African descent as he may think necessary and proper for the suppression of this rebellion." Slaves who enlisted in the Union army would be granted their freedom, while loyal slave owners would be compensated for their losses. Congress also repealed an earlier law that had banned blacks from state militias.

Despite these new measures, the federal government continued to delay black enlistment. Abolitionists who had supported Lincoln's election were furious. Frederick Douglass condemned government leaders for "the pride, the stupid prejudice and folly" that made them reject black volunteers in "this dark and terrible hour."

> [This] is no time to fight with one hand, when both are needed; . . . this is no time to fight only with your white hand, and allow your black hand to remain tied. . . . The national edifice is on fire. Every man who can carry a bucket, or remove a brick, is wanted; but those who have the care of the building, having a profound respect for the feeling of the national burglars who set the building on fire, are determined that the flames shall only be extinguished by Indo-Caucasian [white] hands.

While the Union rejected its black volunteers, Douglass and other abolitionists pointed out, the Confederates were taking full advantage of their slave population. A greater proportion of

THE ABOLITIONIST ARMY

One of the leading abolitionist organizations in Civil War times was the American Anti-Slavery Society. The society had been founded by William Lloyd Garrison in 1833. A mild-looking white man with a thundering voice, Garrison rallied a small but powerful body of allies to the antislavery cause. Among the most prominent leaders of his abolitionist army were Sojourner Truth and Frederick Douglass.

Sojourner Truth was born a slave in New York. After years of cruel treatment under several different masters, she gained her freedom in 1828, when the state abolished slavery. As a leader of the American Anti-Slavery Society, she traveled throughout New England and the West, campaigning for universal freedom and equality. Truth stood nearly six feet tall, and she had a powerful voice. Although she never learned to read or write, her commanding presence and down-to-earth speaking style drew large crowds to her stirring lectures.

Frederick Douglass escaped from slavery in Maryland as a young man. He went on to become a famous writer, lecturer, and newspaper publisher, as well as one of the most influential abolitionists in the nation. His autobiography, *Narrative of the Life of Frederick Douglass, an American Slave,* gave thousands of readers their first "inside" look at a life in bondage. Douglass often introduced himself to audiences as "a thief and a robber. I stole this head, these limbs, this body from my master, and ran off with them."

Above left and right: Sojourner Truth and Frederick Douglass drew on their experiences of slavery to persuade others to support the abolitionist cause.

white men could go to war in the South than in the North because they left behind slaves to carry on the work in factories, shops, and fields. That labor in turn fed and clothed the Confederate army. "Why, in the name of all that is rational, does our Government allow its enemies this powerful advantage?" asked Frederick Douglass. "Arrest that hoe in the hands of the negro, and you smite rebellion in the very seat of its life."

THE EMANCIPATION PROCLAMATION

In August 1861 General John C. Fremont, abolitionist commander of Union forces in Missouri, issued a proclamation freeing all slaves in the state who were owned by supporters of the Confederacy. Concerned that the general's actions would turn the loyal slaveholders of Missouri against the Union, President Lincoln quickly revoked the order. The following spring General David Hunter declared that slaves in South Carolina, Georgia, and Florida were free. Again Lincoln overruled his general's proclamation. When abolitionists criticized his actions, the president repeated his long-standing policy: While he personally hated slavery, his "paramount objective [was] to save the Union, and . . . not either to save or destroy slavery."

Despite all these discouraging developments, it was clear to abolitionists that the Union could not be saved without the overthrow of slavery. As the war dragged on, that point of view began to take hold throughout the North. Even opponents of abolition could see that enlisting blacks would save the lives of white soldiers. Expanding the Union army with black regiments also might hasten the war's end. The black troops would strengthen the army, while freeing the slaves would cripple the

Southern economy, making it much harder for the Confederates to continue their fight.

President Lincoln was encouraged by the shift in public opinion. He was also frustrated by continuing military setbacks and the Confederates' refusal to give up their claims to independence. Finally, he decided that the time was right for a decisive move against slavery. In April 1862 Lincoln asked Congress to pass a bill freeing all slaves in Washington, DC. On the day of emancipation, the editor of *The Anglo-African* newspaper rejoiced, "We can point to our Capital and say to all nations, 'IT IS FREE.'"

Three months later, Lincoln informed his cabinet that he intended to issue a broader emancipation proclamation. On the advice of his closest counselors, the president agreed to wait for a Union military victory. That way his announcement would not be interpreted as "our last shriek on the retreat."

The opportunity came on September 17, 1862, with the Union defeat of a Confederate army at Antietam Creek in Sharpsburg, Maryland. Five days after the Battle of Antietam, President Lincoln issued the preliminary Emancipation Proclamation, warning the Confederates that slavery would be abolished if they did not end their rebellion by the year's end.

On January 1, 1863, Lincoln fulfilled his pledge. The Emancipation Proclamation decreed that "all persons held as

Union troops cheer their commander, General George B. McClellan, at the Battle of Antietam.

slaves" in the rebellious Southern states were "forever free." Further, the document declared that from that point on, freed slaves would be "received into the armed service of the United States."

A "TIME OF TIMES"

The Emancipation Proclamation freed only the slaves in areas in rebellion against the Union. Slaves in the loyal border states remained in bondage. So did slaves owned by masters in a few places in the Confederacy that had resumed their allegiance to the Union. Despite these limitations, the proclamation was a giant step toward abolition. It showed that the North had accepted the idea that victory over the Confederacy depended on the destruction of slavery. It transformed a struggle to

President Abraham Lincoln reads a draft of the Emancipation Proclamation to members of his cabinet.

restore the old Union into a war for a new nation where all would be free.

White Southerners condemned Lincoln's proclamation. Confederate president Jefferson Davis called it the "most execrable [detestable] measure recorded in the history of guilty man." Among white Northerners, reactions were mixed. Many people supported the president and hoped that freeing the slaves would help end the war. Some critics argued that the proclamation did not go far enough, while those who opposed abolition felt betrayed by the president's actions. Some men resigned from the army rather than fight to free the slaves. One angry soldier from Kentucky maintained that the men in his regiment had "volunteered to fight to restore the Old Constitution and not to free the Negroes . . . and we are not a-going to do it."

Among African Americans the verdict was unanimous. The Emancipation Proclamation was a beacon of joy and promise. On December 31, 1862, free black men, women, and children across the North attended "watch meetings," where prayers

Some African Americans greeted the news of emancipation with cheers and songs, others with quiet joy and thankfulness.

were offered for the deliverance of the slaves. The next day thousands gathered to hear readings of the historic document. Henry Turner, the African-American pastor of a church in Washington, DC, stood among a crowd on Pennsylvania Avenue as another man read the proclamation aloud "with great force and clearness."

> While he was reading every kind of demonstration and gesticulation was going on. Men squealed, women fainted, dogs barked, white and colored people shook hands, songs were sung, and by this time cannons began to fire at the navy-yard. . . . Great processions of colored and white men marched to and fro and passed in front of the White House and congratulated President Lincoln on his proclamation. The president came to the window and made responsive bows, and thousands told him, if he would come out of that palace, they would hug him to death. . . . It was indeed a time of times, . . . and nothing like it will ever be seen again in this life.

Fugitive slave John Goosberry risked his safety and freedom to join the regimental band of the Fifty-fourth Massachusetts Volunteers.

Chapter 4

FIGHTING FOR THE UNION

In February 1863 the Union army opened a recruiting office for black soldiers in New Bedford, Massachusetts. One of the first men to enlist in the Fifty-fourth Regiment of Massachusetts Volunteers was James Henry Gooding. Gooding was an experienced seaman who had spent several years as a cook and steward aboard whaling and merchant vessels. Now he was excited by the opportunity to serve the cause of freedom and equality by fighting with the "glorious 54th." As the regiment prepared to depart for training camp, he wrote to a local newspaper, urging other "colored men here in New Bedford" to "embrace probably the only opportunity that will ever be offered them to make themselves a people."

Black Men to Arms

When the Emancipation Proclamation opened the door to black enlistment, African Americans stepped right through. In the early months of 1863, free black men flocked to recruiting stations in Boston, New York, Philadelphia, and other Northern cities. Soon runaway slaves from Union-occupied parts of the Confederacy were signing up, too. Then thousands of men from the border states, including both contrabands and freeborn blacks, joined the fight.

All these black soldiers would serve in segregated units, known as the United States Colored Troops. In May 1863 the Department of War created a new agency, the U.S. Bureau of Colored Troops, to oversee the recruitment and organization of black regiments. By year's end, fifty-eight black regiments were ready for action, and dozens more were being formed.

African-American military service became a powerful force in the destruction of slavery. Slaves were emancipated when they enlisted. In turn, black soldiers helped liberate tens of thousands of slaves as the Union army swept through the South. When Union troops captured a plantation in Confederate territory, most of the women and children were sent to contraband camps, while the able-bodied men were enlisted. Commanders also sent raiding parties of black soldiers to nearby towns and plantations to encourage the slaves to escape their masters and join the army. Slave owners were infuriated by the raids, but most were too intimidated by the armed troops to do anything but shout threats and insults from a safe distance.

Slaves were also recruited as Union troops engaged in military missions throughout the Confederate countryside. In 1863 slaves working in rice fields beside the Combahee River in

Fugitive slaves make their way to a U.S. patrol vessel. Thousands of Southern black men, after escaping from slavery, joined the Union army.

South Carolina were startled by the approach of iron ships filled with blue-coated soldiers. The Union ships had been sent to destroy railroads and bridges, cutting off supplies to the rebel troops. Among the workers, however, word quickly spread that "Lincoln's gun-boats" had come to set them free. Braving the whips of their overseers, eight hundred slaves raced to the river and crowded aboard the liberating vessels.

In the border states, dealing with all the fugitive slaves who wanted to enlist was a delicate problem at first. Before long, though, the army's need for new recruits outweighed the fear of offending loyal slaveholders. In October 1863 the War Department issued an order permitting the recruitment of border-state slaves. Masters who were loyal to the Union would be paid three hundred dollars for each slave who enlisted. In some border states, that was the beginning of the end for slavery. In 1864 Maryland passed a new constitution abolishing slavery, and Missouri soon followed.

THE TEST OF BATTLE

While most white Northerners had accepted the idea of enlisting African Americans in the army, many were not convinced that black soldiers would stand up to a fight. As one New York

SERVING THE CONFEDERACY

From the beginning of the Civil War, there were a number of African Americans who worked not for the Union but for the Confederacy. While most were slaves who had been compelled into labor, free Southern blacks also offered their services to the Confederate army. Some volunteered out of loyalty to their former masters or communities. Others were pressured by local officials. A group of free African Americans in New Orleans told Union soldiers who captured the city in 1862 that "they had not dared to refuse; that they had hoped, by serving the Confederates, to advance a little nearer to equality with whites."

Southern war leaders were glad to take advantage of African-American labor, but they did not seriously consider enlisting black soldiers until late 1864. By that time, nearly four years of fighting had left the Southern army in tatters. New troops were urgently needed, and the success of black Union regiments had convinced the Confederates that African Americans could make good soldiers. Yet even in that desperate hour, there were still many Southerners who opposed the idea of arming the slaves. The Confederacy had been founded on the principle that blacks were an inferior race, born to serve white masters. As one Southern general pointed out, "If slaves will make good soldiers our whole theory of slavery is wrong."

In March 1865 Jefferson Davis signed the Negro Slave Act. Under the new law, slaves who joined the Confederate army would be granted their freedom, as long as their owners and state governments consented. While a small number of slaves took advantage of the offer and enlisted, the war would be over before any black regiments could be formed.

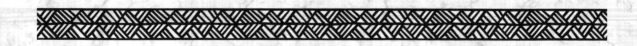

newspaper reported, "Loyal Whites have generally become willing that [black men] should fight, but the great majority have no faith that they will really do so. Many hope that they will prove cowards and sneaks—others greatly fear it."

African Americans were eager to prove the skeptics wrong. At first, however, black regiments were assigned to hard labor rather than combat. While white soldiers drilled, rested, and marched off to fight, blacks hauled logs, dug trenches, built fortifications, loaded and unloaded supplies, and buried the dead. "Instead of the musket It is the spad[e] and the Whelbarrow and the Axe," complained one weary enlisted man from Louisiana.

Finally, in late May 1863, black troops got their first chance to prove their courage under fire. Two black regiments, the First and Third Louisiana Native Guards, joined white troops in an attack on Port Hudson, a Confederate stronghold on the lower Mississippi River. Although the attack ended in failure, the black soldiers performed heroically, charging over open ground under heavy artillery and rifle fire. The *New York Times* proclaimed that the "awful ordeal" had settled "the question that the negro race can fight. . . . The men, white or black, who will not flinch from that will flinch from nothing."

Eleven days later, three regiments of former slaves helped beat back a Confederate assault on Milliken's Bend, a Union outpost in Louisiana. When their guns failed, the African-American soldiers engaged the enemy in fierce hand-to-hand combat, battling with fists, bayonets, and rifle butts. One Southern officer reported that his men's charge was "resisted by the negro portion of the enemy's force with considerable obstinacy, while the white or true Yankee portion ran like whipped curs [dogs]."

Colonel Robert Gould Shaw commanded the Fifty-fourth Massachusetts Volunteers, the first regiment of free blacks organized in the North.

Then came the battle that would establish once and for all the bravery and resolve of black soldiers. On July 18, 1863, the Fifty-fourth Regiment of Massachusetts Volunteers was chosen to lead an assault on Fort Wagner in South Carolina. The first regiment of free blacks organized in the North, the Fifty-fourth was made up of about six hundred men, including two of Frederick Douglass's sons and a grandson of Sojourner Truth. Its commander was twenty-six-year-old Robert Gould Shaw, the son of prominent white abolitionists.

A narrow stretch of sand led to Fort Wagner. As the men of the Fifty-fourth crossed the beach, they fell under a murderous hail of musket and artillery fire. Those who survived the crossing plunged through a watery ditch, then scrambled up a high earthen wall toward the rebel fortifications. Enemy fire swept through the rapidly thinning ranks, but the soldiers pressed on. At last the men reached the top of the wall. There they faced the enemy's bayonets and rifles. Hopelessly outnumbered, the survivors were finally forced to pull back.

The regiment had lost 272 men, or nearly half its force, including its young commander. The attack had failed, but in a larger sense it was a historic victory. The New York *Tribune* summed up its significance:

It is not too much to say that if this Massachusetts Fifty-fourth had faltered when its trial came, two hundred thousand colored troops for whom it was a pioneer would never have been put into the field. . . . But it did not falter. It made Fort Wagner such a name to the colored race as Bunker Hill has been for nearly ninety years to the white Yankees.

Two days after the assault on Fort Wagner, James Henry Gooding wrote this account: "We went at it over the ditch and on to the parapet through a deadly fire; but we could not get into the fort. We met the foe on the parapet of Wagner with the bayonet—we were exposed to a murderous fire from the batteries of the fort, from our Monitors [ships] and our land batteries. . . . Mortal men could not stand such a fire. . . . It is not for us to blow our horn, but when a regiment of white men gave us three cheers as we were passing them, it shows that we did our duty as men should."

The Fifty-fourth Massachusetts storms Fort Wagner on July 18, 1863. One survivor wrote to his mother, "They mowed us down like grass."

BATTLING ON TWO FRONTS

From their first fight, it was clear that African-American troops faced even greater perils than whites on the field of battle. Blacks who were captured by the enemy were often treated not like soldiers but like slaves guilty of rebellion. While some African-American captives were held in prisoner-of-war camps, many others were executed, and a few were sold into slavery. Following the battles of Port Hudson and Milliken's Bend, the Confederates hanged a number of black prisoners. In retaliation President Lincoln threatened to execute one rebel soldier for each Union soldier killed "in violation of the laws of war." Still, the war crimes continued. The worst took place at Fort Pillow, a small Union outpost in Tennessee. In April 1864

THE NEW YORK DRAFT RIOTS

This man's whipped back is evidence of the violent attacks on African Americans during the New York Draft Riots of 1863.

Racial prejudice and job competition between white and black laborers led to wartime attacks on African Americans in several Northern cities. The worst violence took place in New York City, following congressional passage of the nation's first draft law in March 1863. The law required all able-bodied males between the ages of twenty and forty-five to serve in the Union army. It also permitted men to escape service by hiring a substitute or paying a three-hundred-dollar fee. Working-class whites were outraged. Free blacks already had taken many of the low-paying jobs once reserved for white workers. Now, while rich men bought their way out of the service, poor whites would have to fight to free slaves who were likely to come north and provide even more job competition. The headline of one newspaper reflected the prejudice widespread among Northern whites:

WILLING TO FIGHT FOR UNCLE SAM BUT NOT FOR UNCLE SAMBO.

On July 13, 1863, when the names of the first draftees were drawn in New York City, a mob of mostly Irish workingmen and women burned down the draft office. Then the rioters stormed through the city streets. They attacked African-American men, destroyed homes and stores where blacks lived and worked, and set fire to an orphanage for black children. By the time order was restored three days later, the riots had killed or wounded hundreds of people and caused an estimated $1.5 million to $2 million in property damage.

the Confederates captured the fort and massacred hundreds of unarmed black soldiers who had surrendered. Some of the victims were burned alive.

The Confederate atrocities did not stop African Americans from fighting with spirit and determination. In fact, the knowledge that they fought with "ropes 'round their necks" may have inspired black troops to even greater ferocity. According to one white soldier from Pennsylvania, Southern troops were "not as much afraid of us as they are of the [black troops]. When they charge they will not take any prisoners, if they can help it. Their cry is, 'Remember Fort Pillow!'"

African-American soldiers faced abuse and prejudice not only from the enemy but from within the Union army, too. They were assigned far more than their share of hard labor. They were often issued spoiled food, poorly made uniforms, and inferior equipment, including guns that would not fire and bayonets that did not fit their muskets. While medical care was primitive for all soldiers in Civil War times, black troops were routinely tended by the least competent doctors, equipped with inadequate supplies. In addition, nearly all African-American regiments were commanded by white officers, and even the most skilled black soldier had little chance of rising through the ranks. Perhaps worst of all, African Americans were treated with tremendous contempt. They endured ugly racial insults and even physical brutality from white Northern soldiers. Black men who complained or spoke out were often punished and imprisoned.

On top of all these abuses, African-American soldiers were paid less than whites. White privates earned $13.00 a month plus a $3.50 clothing allowance. Blacks received $10.00, from which $3.00 was *deducted* for clothing. Several black regiments served for nearly a year without pay after refusing to accept the discriminatory smaller wages. The commander of one of these regiments wrote to his state's governor, defending his men's right to be paid "according to the terms of their enlistment. They would rather work and fight . . . without any pay, than accept from the Government less than it gives to other soldiers from Massachusetts."

In June 1864 Congress passed a law granting black soldiers equal pay. Men who had been free before the war started were awarded back payment to the time they enlisted. However, former slaves would receive their lost wages only back to January 1, 1864. A group of former slaves in a South Carolina regiment continued to refuse payment until that injustice, too, was corrected. In March 1865, a month before the war's end, Congress passed a second law, granting former slaves all their back pay.

The men of the Fifty-fourth Massachusetts had been in the army for five months when they were called out to receive their first paychecks. Explaining that there had been "a little financial hitch," a white officer offered them three dollars less than the thirteen dollars they had been promised when they enlisted. "I am glad to say," wrote James Henry Gooding, "that not one man in the whole regiment lifted a hand" to accept the offer. In a letter to President Lincoln, Gooding asked, "We have done a Soldier's Duty. Why Can't we have a Soldier's pay? . . . The Regt. do pray that they be assured their service will be fairly appreciated by paying them as American Soldiers, not as menial hirelings."

That appeal was answered nearly a year later, when Congress equalized the pay of white and black soldiers. In September 1864,

$170,000 in back pay was distributed to the Fifty-fourth Massachusetts. It came too late for James Henry Gooding. Wounded and captured during a battle with Confederate forces, he had been sent to a prisoner-of-war camp, where he died on July 19, 1864.

A PROUD LEGACY

By the end of the Civil War, about 180,000 African Americans had served in the Union army, making up nearly one-tenth of all Northern troops. Black soldiers participated in every major military campaign after the middle of 1863. More than 38,000 gave their lives in the service of their country. Eighteen were awarded the Congressional Medal of Honor, the nation's highest award for courage in action against an enemy force.

Major Martin Robinson Delany received the Congressional Medal of Honor for heroism during the Civil War.

"If we hadn't become soldiers, all might have gone back as it was before," reflected one former slave late in the war. "But now things can never go back, because we have shown our energy and our courage and our . . . manhood." Black troops had endured great hardships, but for the most part their service was an overwhelmingly positive experience. Many soldiers had learned to read and write in regimental schools. Their successful fight for equal pay had taught them valuable lessons in securing the rights of citizenship. The sacrifices of those who risked their lives and shed their blood for their country had strengthened the former slaves' claims to freedom. In the postwar years, the memory of black contributions to Union victory would inspire all African Americans in their struggle for full equality.

Chapter 5

SAILORS, SCOUTS, AND SPIES

WHILE BLACK SOLDIERS RECEIVED THE LION'S SHARE OF both the controversy and the glory, African Americans were also contributing to the Union war effort in a number of other areas. Black men served in the Union navy, helping to secure victory at sea. Both men and women, free and enslaved, served the army as scouts and spies. Meanwhile, on the home front, black families struggled to survive in a time of great changes and challenges.

IN THE NAVY

For most of its history, the U.S. Navy had welcomed free black men to its ranks. Soon after the start of the Civil War, contrabands were also encouraged to enlist. A number of former slaves had worked as boatmen in the South's winding coastal

Opposite: Both slaves and free blacks scouted for the Union army, helping Northern troops move safely through Southern territories.

and inland waterways. Union commanders recognized the value of that experience. They also knew that the Confederates were using slaves on their naval ships. "If negroes are to be used in this contest," wrote one Union officer in the summer of 1861, "I have no hesitation they should be used to preserve the government not to destroy it."

An estimated 18,000 African Americans served in the Union navy during the war, making up about 15 percent of all Northern seamen. Black sailors manned the ships that transported troops and supplies, blockaded Southern ports, protected merchant vessels, and engaged the Confederates in battle. Black women worked as nurses aboard U.S. naval vessels. About eight hundred African-American seamen died in action during the war, and seven earned the Congressional Medal of Honor.

Overall, African Americans encountered less racial discrimination in the navy than their counterparts faced in the army. Black and white seamen served side by side, performing the same duties and receiving the same pay. There were few black officers, however, and most black sailors served in the lowest ranks.

One African American who managed to rise through the ranks was Robert Smalls. As a slave in Charleston, South Carolina, Smalls served as the pilot of the Confederate gunboat *Planter*. On nights when the ship sat in Charleston Harbor, he and eight other enslaved crewmen remained on board while the white officers went ashore to their homes. About a year after the Civil War began, Smalls came up with a plan to escape and aid the Union cause.

On May 12, 1862, the *Planter* was loaded with a valuable cargo of military supplies. That night Smalls slipped a number

American naval hero Robert Smalls

of friends and family members aboard. Early the next morning, he eased the *Planter* out of port. As the ship passed under the Confederate guns at Fort Sumter, Smalls saluted with the signal whistle to avoid suspicion. At last the *Planter* reached the open sea. The crew raised a white flag of surrender and headed for the nearest Union vessel. Stepping forward and taking off his cap, Smalls shouted over to the ship's commander, "Good morning, sir! I've brought you some of the old United States guns, sir!"

For their daring deed, Robert Smalls and his men were awarded half the proceeds from the sale of the enemy ship. Smalls enlisted in the navy, with the rank of second lieutenant, and was assigned as pilot to the *Planter,* now a Union vessel. In November 1863 he distinguished himself once again during a fierce battle with Confederate forces. When the *Planter*'s captain considered surrender, Smalls rallied the crew to a spirited defense and saved the ship from capture. The heroic pilot was promoted to the rank of captain. He went on to participate in more than a dozen other engagements, gaining fame as one of the Civil War's greatest naval heroes.

The steam-powered gunboat captured by Smalls and his tiny crew of fugitive slaves

Harriet Tubman, one of the best-known "conductors" on the Underground Railroad, served the Union army as a nurse, scout, and spy.

SECRET AGENTS

Throughout the Civil War, Union commanders operating in the South relied on the services of African-American scouts and spies. Southern blacks knew the countryside better than soldiers from the North. They could travel ahead of the troops and gather information on the location and movements of Confederate forces. Union general Abner Doubleday reported that fugitive slaves brought "much valuable information, which cannot be obtained from any other source. [They] make excellent guides . . . [and] frequently have exposed the haunts of secession spies and traitors."

Some free blacks passed themselves off as slaves to spy for the North. One of the best-known secret agents was Harriet Tubman. Born into slavery in Maryland, Tubman had escaped to freedom through the Underground Railroad. After the war started, she returned south to aid the contrabands on the South Carolina Sea Islands. When the Union army asked Tubman to recruit scouts and spies from among the men on the islands, she not only put together an effective intelligence-gathering network but also personally led several spy missions. Disguising herself as an elderly slave woman, the middle-aged Tubman moved easily through rebel territory, observing the location of Southern troops and supplies.

In July 1863 Harriet Tubman led Union troops on an expedition in South Carolina's Combahee River territory. The soldiers destroyed bridges and railroads, confiscated or destroyed millions of dollars' worth of enemy property, and freed more than 750 slaves. "This is the only military command in America," reported a Union officer, "wherein a woman, black or white, led the raid and under whose inspiration it was originated and conducted."

Mary Elizabeth Bowser was honored as "one of the highest-placed and most productive espionage agents of the Civil War."

Another intrepid Civil War spy was Mary Elizabeth Bowser. Born a slave in Virginia, Bowser had been freed by her owners as a young woman. During the war, she took a job as a servant in the Confederate White House in Richmond, Virginia. As Bowser waited on guests visiting Confederate president Jefferson Davis, she listened to their discussions of military plans and troop movements. While sweeping and dusting, she sneaked a look at telegrams and other military dispatches. She passed along her information to a contact, who conveyed it to Union general Ulysses S. Grant. According to a U.S. Army report, "Jefferson Davis never discovered the leak in his household staff, although he knew the Union somehow kept discovering Confederate plans."

THE UNDERGROUND RAILROAD

The Underground Railroad was a loosely organized network of abolitionists who helped runaway slaves make their way to freedom. By the 1830s, the network had grown from a few scattered operations into a nationwide institution with "stations" as far south as Florida and as far north as Canada. Under the cover of night, "conductors" helped fugitives travel from one station to the next on foot or in covered wagons and other vehicles. During the day, the runaways hid out in barns and attics while the conductor sent word ahead to the next station.

Josiah Henson led more than two hundred slaves to freedom on the Underground Railroad.

Participants in the Underground Railroad included white and black abolitionists, slaves, Native Americans, and members of religious groups such as the Quakers. One of the best-known conductors was Harriet Tubman, who helped about three hundred men, women, and children escape from bondage in Maryland. Another fugitive, John Mason, is believed to have led as many as 1,300 slaves from Kentucky all the way to Canada. At one point Mason was captured and sold back into slavery, but he escaped again to continue his work.

Josiah Henson, who had escaped from a plantation in Kentucky, returned to assist "such of my old friends as had the spirit to make the attempt to free themselves." In his autobiography, *The Life of Josiah Henson,* he described his perilous escape from slavery and his adventures on the Underground Railroad. Many historians believe that Henson's book inspired Harriet Beecher Stowe to write her famous novel *Uncle Tom's Cabin.*

HOMEFRONT PERILS

While some African-American women worked for the Union cause, many others struggled to care for their families amid constant hardships. Most free black families in both the North and South were poor. When black soldiers were denied equal wages, their wives, children, parents, and other dependent relatives suffered. Some families were forced to rely on charity or move to the local poorhouse. Some nearly starved.

Hardest-hit of all were the families of soldiers earning no wages, either because they refused to accept discriminatory pay or due to the army's slow and inefficient accounting systems. "Our families at home are in a suffering condition, and send to their husbands for relief," wrote a black enlisted man whose regiment had gone more than five months without wages. "The Government has never offered us a penny since we have been here. . . . My wife and three little children at home are . . . freezing and starving. She writes to me for aid, but I have nothing to send her."

In the loyal border states where slavery remained legal, black families endured not only poverty but also the threat of abuse from slave owners. While men earned their freedom by enlisting, their wives and children often remained in bondage. A slaveholder embittered by the loss of a good worker might take out his anger by overworking, abusing, or cutting the rations of the man's family. Martha Glover, enslaved in Missouri, told her husband that her master and mistress had given her "nothing but trouble" since he enlisted. "They abuse me because you went," she wrote, and "say they will not take care of our children & do nothing but quarrel with me all the time and beat me scandalously."

To protect their families from such abuses, some African-American soldiers took their families with them when they enlisted. The wives and children of these soldiers lived in crowded contraband camps near the forts or camps where black regiments were stationed. Border-state slaveholders sometimes pursued families who had followed their menfolk to army camps and forced the fugitives back into slavery. A group of white citizens in Missouri reported that slave women and children were "beaten, seized and driven to their former homes in the night."

Some Union commanders refused shelter to the families of black soldiers from the loyal border states, arguing that the slaves' owners were responsible for supporting them. In 1864 General Speed Fry, commander of Camp Nelson in Kentucky, evicted four hundred women and children from a contraband camp that had been set up for the families of black soldiers. On a bitter-cold November morning, the refugees were forced into wagons, transported a few miles, then dumped by the roadside. That night Joseph Miller went in search of his family. Miller was a freedman from Kentucky who had brought along his wife and four children "because my master said that if I enlisted he would not maintain them." He was especially worried about his seven-year-old son, who was recovering from a serious ill-

Students at a "contraband school" in North Carolina. In the midst of great hardships, former slaves like these took their first steps toward freedom.

THE CIVIL WAR

ness. After walking six miles, Miller finally found his family in an old meetinghouse crammed with other refugees.

> The building was very cold having only one fire. My wife and children could not get near the fire because of the number of colored people huddled together by the soldiers. I found my wife and children shivering with cold and famished with hunger. They had not received a morsel of food during the whole day. My boy was dead.

Heartbreaking stories like this would be repeated again and again until the Civil War's end. While the conflict had given hope to millions of African Americans, it had also brought untold misery and peril. Many black men, women, and children suffered and died. Many others found a way to endure and sometimes even to prosper. And all African Americans looked forward to the day when peace would reign and slavery's chains would be forever broken.

Chapter 6

A New Era

BY THE SPRING OF 1865, THE SOUTHERN ARMY WAS ON its last legs. Hundreds of men were deserting every day, discouraged by meager rations, news of hunger and hardships back home, and a recent string of military losses. Even those who remained at their posts longed for peace. "The soldiers are badly out of heart," wrote one Confederate enlisted man in January 1865, "for they have been a suffering for nearly four long years and there is no prospect of doing better."

On April 9, Robert E. Lee, commander of the Confederate army, surrendered to Union general Ulysses S. Grant at Appomattox Court House, Virginia. Tom Hester, a freeborn black man working for the Union army, watched as the two generals "stood there talking about half an hour and then they shake hands and us what was watching know that Lee done

Opposite: An African-American woman poses for her portrait at the start of a new era of hope and freedom.

Springfield, Illinois, shortly after the Lincoln assassination. Signs and banners express the grief of the townspeople over the loss of their most famous inhabitant.

give up. . . . General Lee rode over to the rebel side. General Grant rode over to our side, and the war was over."

Five days later, John Wilkes Booth, an actor and a fanatical Confederate, assassinated President Abraham Lincoln. African Americans were deeply saddened by the loss of the leader who would be immortalized as the Great Emancipator. A black seamstress in Washington, DC, summed up the feelings of many: "The Moses of my people [has] fallen in the hour of his triumph."

THE DAWN OF FREEDOM

The end of the Civil War marked the beginning of a new era in American history. Never again could one American claim the right to hold another in bondage. In January 1865 Congress had approved the Thirteenth Amendment to the U.S. Constitution. When the amendment was ratified by the states, slavery was officially abolished throughout the nation.

Thousands of African Americans had escaped from slavery during the Civil War. Freedom did not come to most slaves, however, until the war's end. When those still in bondage heard about the Confederate surrender, they felt a wide variety of emotions, from bewilderment to disbelief to jubilation. James Lucas, a former slave of Confederate president Jefferson Davis, recalled that he and his friends "didn' know jus' zactly what it meant. . . . Folks dat ain' never been free don' rightly know de *feel* of bein' free." Felix Haywood of Texas described the excitement on the plantation when "the end of the war, it come jus' like that—like you snap your fingers. . . . Everybody was a-singin'. We was all walking on golden clouds. Hallelujah!"

Tom Robinson, also enslaved in Texas, ran to visit a neighboring black family as soon as he heard the news of emancipation. "I wanted to find out if they was free too," he remembered. "I just couldn't take it all in. I couldn't believe we was all free alike." Robinson had always thought of his master as a good man, who "treated me almost like I was one of his own children." Still, as the realization sank in that he was no longer a slave, his heart filled with happiness. "You can take anything," he explained years later. "No matter how good you treat it, it wants to be free. You can treat it good and feed it good and give it everything it seems to want, but if you open the cage, it's happy."

SPREADING THE WORD

In remote areas of the Confederacy, some slaveholders managed to keep the news of emancipation from their slaves for months or even years after the Civil War ended. Susan Merritt did not hear about the defeat of the slave powers until September 1865, when a "Government man" rode up to her master's house in Texas and "read a paper to the slaves telling them they was free." Ben Simpson remained in chains for three years after the war's end, until his master in Texas was hanged for horse stealing. Tempie Cummins recalled that her mother overheard their master "telling missus that the slaves was free but they didn't know it and he's not gwineter tell 'em till he makes another crop or two. When mother hear that . . . she runs to the field . . . and tol' all the other slaves and they quit work."

SLAVE NARRATIVES

In the 1930s interviewers working for the Federal Writers' Project traveled across the South, recording the oral histories of more than two thousand former slaves. One of the voices in those historic recordings belonged to ninety-year-old Ben Simpson.* Born a slave in Georgia, Simpson came under the control of a cruel master named Roger Stielszen. After the Civil War started, Stielszen marched all his slaves to Texas.

He chains all he slaves round the necks and fastens the chains to the hosses and makes them walk all the way to Texas. . . . Mother, she give out on the way. . . . Then Massa, he jus' take out [his] gun and shot her, and whilst she lay dyin' he kicks her two, three times. . . . He wouldn't bury mother, jus' leave her layin' where he shot her. . . .

I swore if I ever got a-loose I'd kill him. But befo' long . . . he fails to come home, and some people finds him hangin' from a tree. Boss, that long after war time he got hung. He didn't let us free. We wore chains all the time. When we work, we drug them chains with us. At night he lock us to a tree to keep us from runnin' off.

After Simpson finally gained his freedom, he went to work as a farmer. In time he married and raised thirteen children. "I not got much time to stay here," the elderly man said at the end of his interview. "I's ready to see God but I hope my old massa ain't there to torment me again."

* You can read Ben Simpson's narrative and the oral histories of about two hundred other former slaves at the Library of Congress Web site *Born in Slavery: Slave Narratives from the Federal Writers' Project, 1936–1938*, at http://memory.loc.gov/ammem/snhtml/snhome.html

Above: Anderson and Minerva Edwards were among the many former slaves interviewed as part of the Federal Writers' Project.

Often the first news of freedom came through African-American soldiers, including many who had been slaves themselves. After the Confederate surrender, most black soldiers spent the remainder of their military service in the occupied South. There they liberated tens of thousands of slaves still laboring on plantations. They restored order, rebuilt devastated towns and cities, and helped black communities organize their first schools, churches, and orphanages. Many soldiers also took on the responsibility of protecting the lives and liberties of newly liberated slaves. E. S. Robison, a black sergeant from Michigan, sent this protest to the top military commander in South Carolina on behalf of a freedman whose appeals to a local official had gone unanswered:

> Andrew Lee a Collord man Come in from the Country to Report some White men for going into his house and Breaking open his trunks with a pretinse of searching for a hog that they Claimed to have lost. . . . After hearing Andrew Lees complaint [the local commander] told Lee to Go off and that he . . . ought to put Lee in the Guard house and that those men had a Wright to search his house. . . . Sir I am only a sergeant and of Course Should be as silent as posible but in this I Could not hold my temper after fighting to get wrights that White men might Respect By Virtue of the Law.

As Sergeant Robison had discovered, even white Northerners who had fought against the slave powers sometimes

African-American soldiers return home after the end of the Civil War.

remained deeply prejudiced against African Americans. To white Southerners, the sight of armed and uniformed black men was intolerable. Some former Confederates took out their resentment against black soldiers with insults, threats, and violence. Some black soldiers were beaten or killed. One African-American sergeant serving in Memphis, Tennessee, reported that he had been clubbed and kicked by two white policemen who threatened to "kill all the Damned [black] Soldiers."

To former slaves, meanwhile, the black troops were heroes and liberators. An African-American sergeant marching with his regiment through the former Confederate capital at Richmond marveled at the crowds who turned out to praise the victorious soldiers. "The change seems almost miraculous," he said. "The very people who, three years ago, crouched at their master's feet, on the accursed soil of Virginia, now march in a victorious column of freedmen, over the same land."

THE ROAD AHEAD

As the freedom celebrations ended and the soldiers went home, African Americans faced a long and difficult journey. Slavery was dead. It was not yet clear, however, what shape freedom would take in a reunited America. Many white Southerners were determined to regain control over blacks. During the postwar era known as Reconstruction, Southern legislatures would pass laws denying former slaves their hard-won rights and liberties. Over the following decades, millions of African Americans would suffer injustice, intimidation, and abuse in their fight for true citizenship.

In the more immediate future, newly freed slaves faced a desperate struggle for financial security. Men and women with little or no experience providing for themselves and their families suddenly had to find jobs, homes, food, and clothing in a war-ravaged region. The U.S. government did little to help them get on their feet. Andrew Johnson, who succeeded Abraham Lincoln as president, opposed efforts to strengthen the Freedmen's Bureau, which had been set up near the war's end to provide aid to the freed slaves. Johnson handed out liberal pardons to former Confederates, who returned to reclaim thousands of acres of land abandoned during the war. Some 40,000 former slaves who had been farming the confiscated lands lost their homes, incomes, and chance of independence. Black veterans and widows of black soldiers had to fight the government to collect their rightful back pay and any pensions that were due to them.

In the midst of all these challenges, former slaves were also busy embracing the benefits of freedom. Parents, children, husbands, and wives who had been separated in slavery searched for

Political cartoonist Thomas Nast condemns President Andrew Johnson for "kicking out" the Freedmen's Bureau.

their missing loved ones. Hoping to reunite their scattered families, they placed ads in newspapers and traveled across the South, tracking down leads. Many former slaves took new names, often naming themselves after their fathers, famous Americans, or other admired people. Some took the names of former masters, hoping that would make it easier for missing family members to find them. Husbands and wives registered their first legal marriages. Parents and children attended school together, eager to get an education and claim their long-denied share of the American dream.

In early 1865 the African-American newspaper *Christian Recorder* issued a call to action that echoed the dreams and determination of millions of newly freed people:

> Lay claim to every available opportunity of amassing property, increasing wealth, becoming stockholders, merchants and mechanics, that our foothold may be strengthened upon the soil of our native land. Let us, en masse, make rapid strides in literary culture and moral improvement. . . . [As] taxpayers, and loyal subjects of a Free Republican Government, let us contend lawfully, rightfully and perseveringly for our political rights. . . . We have feasted on celebrations enough to go on and do a little more work. . . . *No shouting yet! Go on and complete the victory!*

Glossary

abolish Put an end to.

abolitionists People who called for the abolition, or ending, of slavery.

aggrandizement The act of making something greater, wealthier, or more powerful.

arsenal A place where weapons and other military equipment are manufactured or stored.

blockade To shut off, or block, a harbor in order to keep ships and supplies from going in or out.

border states The slaveholding states on the border between North and South, which included Delaware, Kentucky, Maryland, Missouri, and Virginia. Only Virginia joined the Confederacy. The western part of the state declared its independence and joined the Union as West Virginia.

Deep South The southeastern states (usually considered to include Alabama, Georgia, Louisiana, and parts of Mississippi, Arkansas, and Texas) where most slaves lived at the start of the Civil War.

emancipation The act of freeing someone from the control and power of another.

Free-Soil Opposed to the extension of slavery into the western territories of the United States.

fugitives People who flee or try to escape.

gesticulation A forceful gesture or movement.

illiterate Unable to read or write.

imminent Approaching, about to happen.

Louisiana Purchase The U.S. purchase of the Louisiana Territory from France in 1803. The Louisiana Purchase doubled the size of the nation, extending U.S. borders westward from the Mississippi River to the Rocky Mountains and north from the Gulf of Mexico to Canada.

overseer A man who was hired to supervise the slave laborers on a plantation.

parapet An earthen wall built around a fort to protect it from enemy attack.

plantations Large farm estates.

Quakers Members of the Society of Friends, a religious community founded in England. The Quakers in New Jersey and Pennsylvania were among the earliest and most active American abolitionists.

Reconstruction The period after the Civil War during which the Confederate states were readmitted into the Union.

reprieve A temporary delay or release from trouble.

secede To formally withdraw from a group or an organization.

secession The act of seceding.

teamsters People who drive teams of horses or mules for hauling goods.

To Find Out More

Books

Collier, Christopher, and James Lincoln Collier. *Slavery and the Coming of the Civil War, 1831–1861.* New York: Benchmark Books, 2000.

Dudley, William, ed. *American Slavery.* San Diego, CA: Greenhaven Press, 2000.

Edwards, Judith. *Abolitionists and Slave Resistance: Breaking the Chains of Slavery.* Berkeley Heights, NJ: Enslow Publishers, 2004.

Elster, Jean Alicia, ed. *The Outbreak of the Civil War.* San Diego, CA: Greenhaven Press, 2003.

Lester, Julius. *To Be a Slave.* New York: Dial Books, 1998.

McKissack, Patricia C., and Fredrick L. McKissack. *Days of Jubilee: The End of Slavery in the United States.* New York: Scholastic Press, 2003.

McPherson, James M. *Marching Toward Freedom: Blacks in the Civil War, 1861–1865.* New York: Facts on File, 1994.

Mettger, Zak. *Till Victory Is Won: Black Soldiers in the Civil War.* New York: Puffin Books, 1997.

Schomp, Virginia. *Letters from the Battlefront: The Civil War.* New York: Benchmark Books, 2004.

Web Sites

Africans in America. Part Four, The Civil War. WGBH Interactive and PBS Online. Copyright 1998, 1999 WGBH Educational Foundation. http://www.pbs.org/wgbh/aia/part4/4narr5.html

Born in Slavery: Slave Narratives from the Federal Writers' Project, 1936–1938. Library of Congress, 2001.
http://memory.loc.gov/ammem/snhtml/snhome.html

History of African Americans in the Civil War. National Park Service, U.S. Department of the Interior.
http://www.itd.nps.gov/cwss/history/aa_history.htm

The Learning Page: Civil War and Reconstruction, 1861–1877. Library of Congress, 2002.
http://memory.loc.gov/learn/features/timeline/civilwar/civilwar.html

Bibliography

Berlin, Ira. *Generations of Captivity: A History of African-American Slaves.* Cambridge, MA: Harvard University Press, 2003.

Berlin, Ira, Marc Favreau, and Steven F. Miller, eds. *Remembering Slavery: African Americans Talk about Their Personal Experiences of Slavery and Emancipation.* New York: New Press, 1998.

Franklin, John Hope, and Alfred A. Moss Jr. *From Slavery to Freedom: A History of African Americans.* New York: Alfred A. Knopf, 2004.

Gooding, James Henry. *On the Altar of Freedom: A Black Soldier's Civil War Letters from the Front.* Edited by Virginia M. Adams. New York: Warner Books, 1991.

Halpern, Rick, and Enrico Dal Lago, eds. *Slavery and Emancipation.* Malden, MA: Blackwell Publishing, 2002.

Holt, Michael F. *The Fate of Their Country: Politicians, Slavery Extension, and the Coming of the Civil War.* New York: Hill and Wang, 2004.

Horton, James Oliver, and Lois E. Horton. *Slavery and the Making of America.* New York: Oxford University Press, 2005.

Johnson, Charles, and Patricia Smith. *Africans in America: America's Journey through Slavery.* New York: Harcourt Brace, 1998.

Kolchin, Peter. *American Slavery, 1619–1877.* New York: Hill and Wang, 2003.

McPherson, James M. *The Negro's Civil War: How American Blacks Felt and Acted during the War for the Union.* New York: Vintage, 2003.

Schneider, Dorothy, and Carl J. Schneider. *Slavery in America: From Colonial Times to the Civil War.* New York: Facts on File, 2001.

Index

Page numbers for illustrations are in boldface

About the Authors

ANNE DEVEREAUX JORDAN is an author, editor, and the founder and former executive director of the Children's Literature Association. In 1992 the association honored her with the establishment of the Anne Devereaux Jordan Award, now given annually for outstanding contributions in children's literature. Ms. Jordan graduated from the University of Michigan, Ann Arbor, where she received the Avery and Jule Hopwood Awards in Poetry and Short Story. She lives in Mansfield Center, Connecticut, and teaches children's and adolescent literature part-time at Eastern Connecticut State University.

VIRGINIA SCHOMP has written more than fifty titles for young readers on topics including dolphins, dinosaurs, occupations, American history, and world history. She lives in the Catskill Mountain region of New York with her husband, Richard, and their son, Chip.